This book belongs to

....

Thomas & Friends™ Story Treasury

A treasury of 12 favourite stories from the Thomas Story Library Collection

Thomas & Friends™
Story Treasury

With 12 favourite stories

EGMONT

We bring stories to life

First published in Great Britain 2013
by Egmont UK Limited
The Yellow Building, 1 Nicholas Road
London W11 4AN

Thomas the Tank Engine & Friends™

CREATED BY BRITT ALLCROFT

Based on the Railway Series by the Reverend W Awdry
© 2013 Gullane (Thomas) LLC. A HIT Entertainment company.
Thomas the Tank Engine & Friends and Thomas & Friends are trademarks of Gullane (Thomas) Limited.
Thomas the Tank Engine & Friends and Design is Reg. U.S. Pat. & Tm. Off.

978 0 6035 6904 3
55713/1
Printed in China

Contents

The **Troublesome Trucks** are the chief mischief-makers on Sodor. They are often the cause of accidents on the Island and don't mind coming off the rails!

James is a medium-sized tender engine with a scarlet coat of paint and a shiny brass dome. James likes to think of himself as a Really Splendid Engine.

Bulgy is a grumpy double-decker bus. He likes things to go his way, and will tell a lie to get out of trouble! Bulgy has had lots of jobs in his time on Sodor.

Terence is sometimes teased by the other engines because of his caterpillar tracks. But he soon proves how useful he can be when he has to pull them out of tight spots!

Skarloey is a very old engine who works on the Narrow Gauge railway. He is kind and wise and looks after the engines working in the Blue Mountain Quarry.

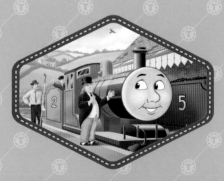

Old **Edward** is a fine and steady tank engine with the same colouring as Thomas. Edward is equally happy pulling coaches or freight along his branch line.

Harold the Helicopter is proud of being able to fly. He is part of the Sodor Rescue Team along with Rocky and Captain, and loves to patrol the Island on rescue missions.

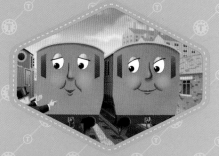

Annie and Clarabel are the most famous carriages on the Island of Sodor. Although they are quite old-fashioned, Thomas wouldn't be without them on his branch line.

Rheneas is a tough little Narrow Gauge engine, but because of his age he often breaks down. He likes to do kind things for his friends, especially Skarloey.

Rocky is the gentle giant of Sodor. He is a very strong crane who wants to be everyone's best friend. Now he works at the Rescue Centre with Harold and Captain.

Jeremy is a jolly jet plane who believes that wings are better than wheels! In times of trouble Jeremy forgets his boastfulness and becomes part of the team.

Hank is a big, bold steam engine with the strength of a giant. Unlike some of the bigger engines, Hank is very kind and helpful, and is willing to offer help to the smaller engines.

Thomas and the Troublesome Trucks

This is a story about the first time
Thomas met the Troublesome Trucks.
Most of the engines knew that the trucks
liked to cause trouble on the railway lines,
but one day Thomas found out for himself …

Thomas the Tank Engine knows how to handle trucks, but the first time he had to pull them wasn't easy.

Soon after he had started working on The Fat Controller's Railway, Thomas became tired of pulling coaches.

"I want to try something different!" he would puff noisily to the engines in the shed every night.

The other engines didn't take much notice. They knew Thomas was young and had a lot to learn.

One night, Edward was next to Thomas in the shed. Edward was
a kind old engine, and felt sorry for Thomas.

"I've got some trucks to pull tomorrow," he told Thomas. "If you
want, you can take them and I'll pull your coaches instead."

"Oh, thank you, Edward!" peeped Thomas, happily.

And all the engines got a good night's sleep, at last!

The next morning, the Drivers agreed to the switch. Thomas puffed off to find Edward's trucks.

He didn't know that trucks were silly, noisy things. They loved to play tricks on engines that didn't know how troublesome they were.

Edward knew all about the trucks. He warned Thomas to be careful, but Thomas was too excited to listen.

Thomas waited impatiently while he was coupled up to the trucks. When the Guard blew his whistle, Thomas quickly peeped in reply and began to puff away. But the trucks didn't want to go. "Oh! Oh!" they screeched. "Wait!"

Thomas wouldn't wait. "Come on, come on," he replied, giving them a hard little bump.

"Ouch!" cried the trucks, as Thomas pulled them onto the Main Line.

Thomas was happy to be doing something different. "Come along, come along," he sang as he went.

"All right, all right," the trucks grumbled.

They clattered through stations and rumbled over bridges. The trucks didn't like being bumped, and looked for a chance to cause trouble for Thomas.

Thomas soon came to the top of Gordon's Hill.

"Steady now," warned his Driver as he shut off steam and put on the brakes. "We're stopping," called Thomas.

"No! No!" said the trucks, naughtily. "Go on! Go on!" Then they all bumped forwards and pushed Thomas down the hill before his Driver could stop them!

Thomas raced down the steep hill much too quickly. The trucks rattled and laughed behind him.

"Stop pushing!" Thomas panted, but the trucks would not stop.

"Huff, huff, ho!
You're too slow.
We'll give you a push
to help you go!" they sang, rudely.

Thomas could see the station at the bottom of the hill, but he was
going too fast to stop. "Cinders and ashes!" he cried.

He whooshed straight past the station platform. The people
waiting there were quite surprised to see a little blue engine going
so fast with a train of laughing trucks.

At the points ahead, Thomas could see that the line split into two tracks. He had an idea. Luckily, the way was clear as he turned off the Main Line and into a goods yard.

"Oh dear! Oh dear!" Thomas groaned, as he skidded along the rails. His brakes screeched and his axles tingled.

At the far side of the yard were the buffers at the end of the track. Thomas was going to crash!

"I must stop!" Thomas said, and his Driver applied the brakes even harder.

The buffers were getting closer and closer. Thomas closed his eyes tight.

But there was no crash.

Thomas opened one eye carefully.

He had stopped just in front of the buffers! But next to the track was The Fat Controller, looking very cross.

"Why did you come in so fast, Thomas?" The Fat Controller boomed.

"I didn't mean to," Thomas explained, meekly. "The trucks pushed me down the hill."

"You've got a lot to learn about trucks, little Thomas," The Fat Controller told him. "You must find a way to make them behave. Then you'll be a Really Useful Engine."

"Yes, Sir!" Thomas promised.

The next day, Edward showed Thomas how to pull the trucks properly and keep them in line when they played their naughty tricks. Thomas even stopped bumping them ... except when they misbehaved.

And from then on, Thomas never complained about his coaches again. They were much easier to pull than those Troublesome Trucks!

James and the Red Coat

This is a story about James the Red Engine.
When he first arrived on Sodor, he was so busy
thinking about his shiny red paint that he soon
got into lots of trouble. The Fat Controller thought
he might have to send him away …

James was a new engine, with a shining coat of red paint.

He had two small wheels in front and six driving wheels behind. They were smaller than Gordon's, but bigger than Thomas'.

"You're a special 'mixed traffic' engine," The Fat Controller told James. "That means you can pull either coaches or trucks."

James felt very proud.

The Fat Controller told James that today he was to help Edward pull coaches.

"You need to be careful with coaches," said Edward. "They don't like getting bumped. If you bump them, they'll get cross."

But James was thinking about his shiny red coat and wasn't really listening.

James and Edward took the coaches to the platform. A group of boys came over to admire James.

"I really am a splendid engine," thought James, and he let out a great *wheeeeeesh* of steam. Everyone jumped, and a shower of water fell on The Fat Controller, soaking his brand-new top hat!

James thought he had better leave quickly before he got into trouble, so he pulled away from the platform.

"Slow down!" puffed Edward, who didn't like starting quickly.

"You're going too fast, you're going too fast," grumbled the coaches.

When James reached the next station, he shot past the platform. His Driver had to back up so the passengers could get off the train.

"The Fat Controller won't be pleased when he hears about this," his Driver said.

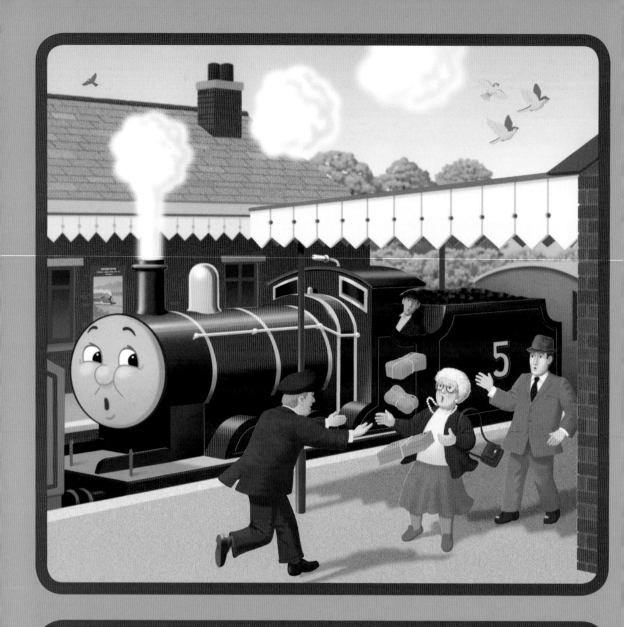

James and Edward set off again, and started to climb a hill.

"It's ever so steep, it's ever so steep," puffed James.

At last they got to the top, and pulled into the next station. James was panting so much that he got hiccups, and frightened an old lady, who dropped all her parcels.

"Oh, dear. The Fat Controller will be even crosser, now!" thought James.

The next morning, The Fat Controller spoke to James very sternly.

"If you don't learn to behave better, I shall take away your red coat and paint you blue!" he warned. "Now run along and fetch your coaches."

James felt cross. "A splendid red engine like me shouldn't have to fetch his own coaches," he muttered.

"I'll show them how to pull coaches," he said to himself, and he set off at top speed. The coaches groaned and protested as they bumped along. But James wouldn't slow down.

At last, the coaches had had enough. "We're going to stop, we're going to stop!" they cried, and try as he might, James found himself going slower and slower. The Driver halted the train and got out. "There's a leak in the pipe," he said. "You were bumping the coaches hard enough to make a leak in anything!"

The Guard made all the passengers get out of the train. "You, sir, please give me your bootlace," he said to one of them. "No, I shan't!" said the passenger. "Well then, we shall just have to stop where we are," said the Guard.

So the man agreed to give his bootlace to the Guard. The Guard used the lace to tie a pad of newspapers round the hole to stop the leak. Now James was able to pull the train again. But he knew he was going to be in real trouble with The Fat Controller this time.

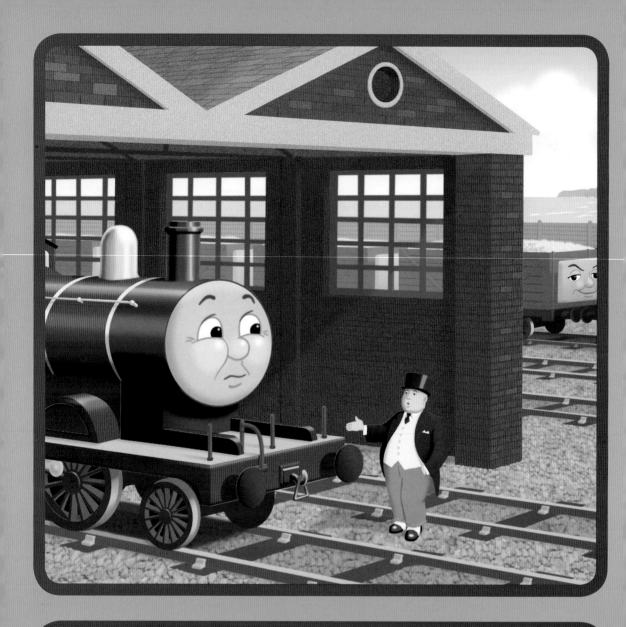

When James got back, The Fat Controller was very angry with him indeed.

For the next few days, James was left alone in the shed in disgrace. He wasn't even allowed to push coaches and trucks in the Yard. He felt really sad. Then one morning, The Fat Controller came to see him. "I see you are sorry," he said to James. "So I'd like you to pull some trucks for me."

"Thank you, Sir!" said James, and he puffed happily away.

"Here are your trucks, James," said a little engine. "Have you got some bootlaces ready?" And he chuffed off, laughing rudely.

"Oh! Oh! Oh!" said the trucks as James backed down on them. "We want a proper engine, not a Red Monster."

James took no notice, but pulled the screeching trucks out of the Yard.

James started to heave the trucks up the hill, puffing and panting.
But halfway up, the last ten trucks broke away and rolled back
down again. James' Driver shut off the steam. "We'll have to go
back and get them," he said to James.

James backed carefully down the hill to collect the trucks.
Then with a 'peep peep' he was off again.

"I can do it, I can do it," he puffed, then … "I've done it,
I've done it," he panted as he climbed over the top.

When James got back to the station, The Fat Controller was very pleased with him. "You've made the most Troublesome Trucks on the line behave," he said. "After that, you deserve to keep your red coat!"

James was really happy. He knew he was going to enjoy working on The Fat Controller's Railway!

Bulgy and the Low Bridge

This is a story about Bulgy the Bus.
He came to work on the Island of Sodor
during the busy season. He thought he was
better than all the engines, so he tried to take
their passengers away …

It was the sightseeing season on the Island of Sodor. The Fat Controller's engines were working hard. Their station was crowded with people.

Duck, Donald and Douglas were taking passengers from the station to other parts of the Island. Some passengers had been brought to Sodor by a big, red bus called Bulgy.

Bulgy looked at the crowded platform and frowned.

"I wouldn't have brought more passengers if I'd known how many were here already," he said.

"But they are all really enjoying themselves," said Duck.

"Pah!" replied Bulgy, crossly.

Duck thought Bulgy was very moody.

Bulgy was rude to all the engines. Every time he saw them, he shouted, "Down with the railways!" He said railways should be closed so coaches, buses and cars could do everything instead!

The engines thought Bulgy was rather silly. But when another bus arrived to take Bulgy's passengers home, the engines were worried. This meant Bulgy was going to stay on the Island. Would he really get the railway closed down? What would the engines do then?

Bulgy told the passengers that he could get them to the Big Station faster than the engines could.

"That's rubbish!" said Duck. "It's much further by road."

"Yes," said Oliver, "but Bulgy says he knows a short cut."

That evening, Duck was about to start his final journey of the day, but he only had a few passengers aboard. He waited for a few minutes, hoping more would turn up, but none did.

Just then, Duck heard a loud, "Toot! Toot!" Bulgy was leaving the station. He had a sign on his side saying 'RAILWAY BUS'. Most of Duck's passengers had gone with Bulgy because he had told them he was working for the railway.

"Stop!" called the railway staff, as Bulgy pulled away, but it was too late.

"Yah! Boo! Snubs!" Bulgy said, as he roared away with the passengers.

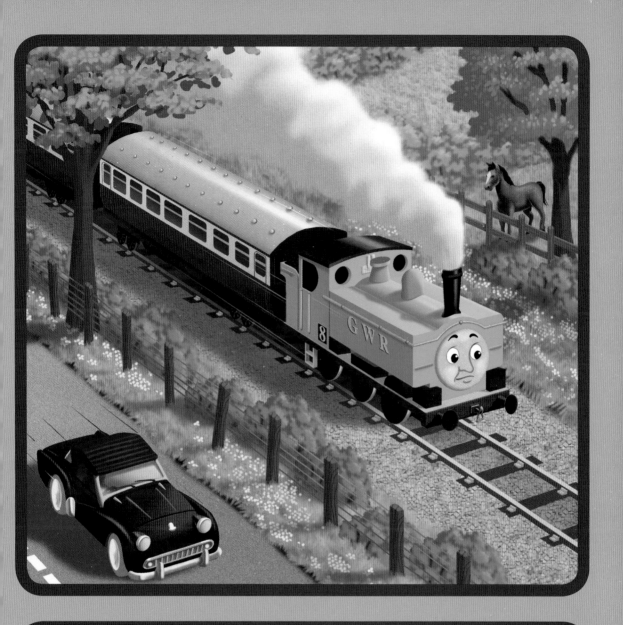

Duck and his carriages, Alice and Mirabel, set off on their journey with the few passengers they had.

"Bulgy is a nasty old thief!" said Alice to Mirabel. "He's taken our people."

Duck knew they had to stop Bulgy taking their passengers. If it carried on like this, the railway could be shut down! He wondered what they should do.

But Bulgy was about to be stopped. His short cut led down
a narrow road with a low bridge. As he rushed under the bridge,
there was a sudden screeching noise and he ground to a halt.
He tried to move forwards and he tried to move backwards but
it was no good. He was totally stuck! Cars and coaches beeped
angrily at Bulgy because he was blocking the road.

"A tall bus like you should never have gone down this road!"
they said.

Bulgy's passengers were furious.

"We should have gone with Duck!" they said. "He would never have let us down like this. We're going to miss our train at the Big Station and it's all your fault," they shouted at Bulgy.

Bulgy didn't say a word.

As Duck reached the bridge, a man appeared by the track, waving a red warning flag.

"Danger!" he cried. "A bus is stuck under the bridge."

Duck moved slowly forward. He saw Bulgy under the bridge.

"So, that is Bulgy's so-called short cut!" he laughed.

Bulgy held his breath as Duck slowly moved over the bridge.

"The bus tricked us!" said Bulgy's passengers. "He said he was working for the railway, but he lied! Can we go with you instead?"

Duck agreed and took all the passengers to the Big Station in time for their train. The passengers promised they would always travel by train from then on.

Bulgy was left under the bridge. He had to wait all night before he was rescued. He didn't learn his lesson though; he still thought he could take over the railway.

But by then, everyone knew that it was faster to go by train so they all travelled with the engines instead.

Bulgy decided to retire. He asked a farmer if he could live in his field and look after his hens. The farmer agreed.

From that day on, Bulgy was much happier. The hens enjoyed hearing about his grand adventures on the bus route, and how terrible engines were. They didn't know any better! And Bulgy felt proud because the hens produced more eggs than ever before.

Terence and the Caterpillar Tracks

This is a story about Terence the Tractor.
When Thomas met Terence ploughing a field,
Thomas was very rude to him. But when snow
came to Sodor, he found out that Terence's
caterpillar tracks could be Really Useful!

Autumn had arrived on the Island of Sodor. The leaves were changing from green to brown, and the fields were changing, too – from yellow stubble to brown earth. As Thomas puffed along, he heard the 'chug chug chug' of a tractor at work, close by.

"Hello!" said Thomas to the tractor. "I'm Thomas. I'm pulling a train."

"Hello!" said the tractor. "My name's Terence. I'm ploughing."

"What ugly wheels you've got!" said Thomas.

"They're not ugly – they're called caterpillars," said Terence. "I can go anywhere. I don't need rails."

"I don't want to go just anywhere," replied Thomas, huffily. "I like my rails, thank you very much."

The next time Thomas saw Terence ploughing a field, he called out to him: "You've missed a bit – over there in the corner! Silly old tractor." And he whistled rudely.

Terence carried on ploughing and didn't reply.

Winter came, and with it, dark, heavy clouds full of snow.

A snow plough was fixed to Thomas, but it was heavy and uncomfortable and he hated it. He shook it and banged it until it was so dented that eventually it had to be taken off.

"You're a very naughty engine!" said his Driver, as he shut the shed door that night.

The next morning, the Driver and Fireman worked hard to mend the snow plough, but they couldn't make it fit properly. So Thomas set out without it. "I don't need that stupid old thing," he said to himself. "Snow is silly soft stuff. It won't stop me."

But as Thomas rode along, the snow made his wheels spin. He passed Terence in a field. "You seem to be having some trouble there," called out Terence. "If you had caterpillars, the snow wouldn't bother you!" This time, it was Thomas who didn't reply.

"Silly soft stuff! Silly soft stuff!" puffed Thomas as he continued on his journey – and he rushed into a tunnel. At the other end, he saw a heap of snow fallen from the sides of the cutting.

"Stupid old snow," said Thomas, and charged it.

"Cinders and ashes!" said Thomas as he ground to a halt. "I'm stuck!"

And he was.

"Oh, my wheels and coupling rods!" said Thomas, sadly. "I shall have to stay here till I'm frozen." And he began to cry.

Just then, who should come chugging along, but Terence the Tractor.

"I heard you were in trouble," said Terence. "So I've come to help."

First, Terence pulled Annie and Clarabel away from the snow drift.

"Thank you, Terence. Thank you, Terence," they said. They were very relieved to be free of the snow, and were sorry that Thomas had been so rude to Terence.

Next, Terence came back for Thomas. He pulled and pulled, but Thomas was buried so deeply in the snow that Terence wasn't strong enough to move him.

"I shall never escape," thought Thomas sadly.

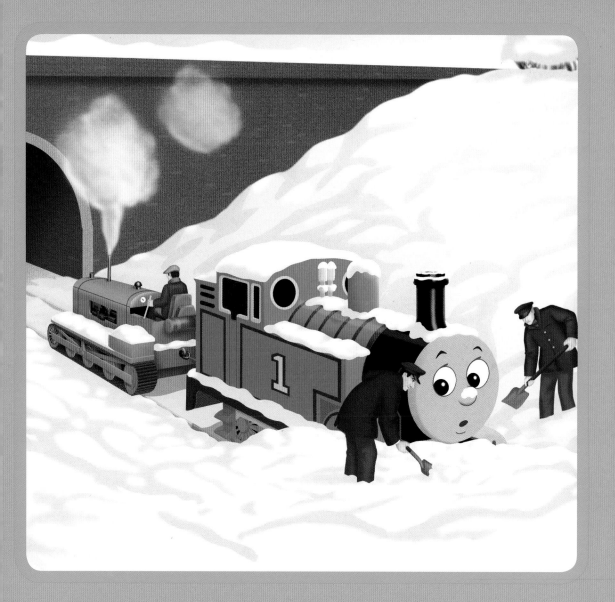

The Driver and Fireman tried to dig the snow away from Thomas; but as fast as they dug, more snow slipped down.

At last Thomas' wheels were clear. But they still spun helplessly when he tried to move.

Terence tugged and slipped, and slipped and tugged. And eventually, with the most enormous effort, he dragged Thomas clear of the snow and into the tunnel.

Thomas was very grateful. "Thank you, Terence," he said.
"I think your caterpillars are splendid. I'm sorry I was so rude
to you before."

"My caterpillars are certainly useful," said Terence. "But I
can't go very fast. I couldn't pull a passenger train like you can,
Thomas."

"Well, my wheels wouldn't be much use for ploughing a field!"
replied Thomas.

And with that, Terence returned to his farm, while Thomas puffed tiredly back to the engine shed.

From then on, Terence and Thomas were good friends. Whenever they passed each other, they always exchanged a cheerful greeting – and they were never rude to each other again!

Skarloey and the Big Bounce

This is a story about Skarloey
the Narrow-Gauge Engine. Skarloey first came
to The Fat Controller's railway 100 years ago.
Read about the troubles he had when
he was brand new – and couldn't stop
bouncing up and down!

Skarloey worked on the Little Railway, on the Island of Sodor.

He was 100 years old, but he was still a Useful Engine. All the other engines liked Skarloey and he would tell them stories about when he was young.

Everyone's favourite story was about the time Skarloey first came to the Little Railway.

Skarloey was built at the same time as another engine called Rheneas. They were both red, with four wheels each. "We look wonderful," said Skarloey, proudly.

"Everyone will want to ride in our coaches!" replied Rheneas.

Skarloey and Rheneas were both going to work on the Little Railway. But Skarloey was finished first, so he had to go to the Little Railway alone. The two engines felt sad when they said goodbye to each other.

Skarloey was sent away on a ship. It was very wobbly!

At the port they used the ship's cranes to lift Skarloey onto the shore. The ship's cranes were called 'derricks', and they nearly turned Skarloey upside down.

"How dare they treat me like this!" said Skarloey, crossly.

He was left hanging from the derricks for a long time. At last an engine arrived to take him to the mountain line.

"About time!" huffed Skarloey.

It was dark when Skarloey arrived at the mountain line. He felt lonely and miserable. "I wish Rheneas was here," he said, sadly.

Next morning there were trucks everywhere. They rattled and roared past Skarloey.

"There's no engine pulling them!" said Skarloey in surprise.

"The trucks come down the mountain by gravity," explained the Manager. "But the empty ones need taking up again. That's why you've come."

"What?" said Skarloey, crossly. "I don't want to pull trucks! Can't I pull coaches, Sir?"

"Certainly not," said the Manager. "We have to finish building this line, and for that, we need trucks. The Inspector is coming to look at the line soon."

Skarloey was furious. When the workmen tried to start him, his fire wouldn't burn. He made no steam – he just blew smoke at them. They tried again the next day, and the next, and the next.

But Skarloey wouldn't do a thing!

Finally, the Manager lost his temper. "We're not going to look at your sulky face all day, Skarloey," he said. "We'll leave you alone until you're a better engine."

They covered Skarloey with a big sheet of tarpaulin and went away. Skarloey felt even more lonely and unhappy. Nobody talked to him.

At last the Manager came back. "I hope that you will be a better engine from now on," he said.

"Yes, Sir, I will, Sir!" said Skarloey, earnestly.

From then on, Skarloey worked very hard, and although he sometimes got too excited and would bounce up and down, the Manager was very pleased with his efforts.

By the time Rheneas arrived at last, the line was ready. Skarloey was delighted to see his old friend!

Rheneas soon settled in. One day, while he was shunting trucks, Skarloey hurried up to him. "I'm going to pull the Inspector's train, today!" said Skarloey.

"Be careful not to bounce," said Rheneas. "The Inspector won't like that."

But Skarloey was so excited, he just couldn't stop bouncing!

Skarloey had to take the Inspector up to the top of the mountain, and then back down again.

The upward journey went well and Skarloey felt very happy.

When it was time to go down, Skarloey was really excited. As they went faster and faster, he began to bounce! The coaches were scared. "He's playing tricks!" they said. "Bump him! Bump him!"

Just then, Skarloey gave an extra big bounce, and the Inspector lost his footing. He flew into a bush on the side of the line!

The Driver stopped the train. The Inspector was not hurt, but he was very cross!

"From now on, you will stay in the shed!" he said to Skarloey. "You are a bad engine!"

When the Inspector told the Manager what had happened, the Manager felt sorry for Skarloey. He knew that he had been trying very hard to be good.

"What Skarloey needs is an extra pair of wheels," he said. "Then he won't bounce any more."

So Skarloey was sent off to the Works.

When Skarloey came back, Rheneas hardly recognised him. He had six wheels and a brand-new cab, and he looked very smart.

"Now let's see what you can do," said the Manager. Sure enough, Skarloey found it much easier to travel along smoothly, without bouncing.

From then on, Skarloey pulled coaches and trucks up and down the track as easily as anything, and he didn't bounce his passengers once! And 100 years later, he is still as good as new!

Edward and the Runaway Engine

This is a story about Edward the Blue Engine.
As an older engine, he could be noisy
and rather slow. The big engines called him names,
but Edward soon had the chance to prove
there was more to him than 'Old Iron' …

Edward was getting old. His parts were worn and the big engines called him 'Old Iron' because he clanked as he worked.

One day, he was taking some empty cattle trucks to the market.

"Come on! Come on! Come on!" puffed Edward, as he clanked along the line.

"Oh! Oh! Oh!" screamed the rattling trucks. Some cows were grazing in a field by the line. When Edward clattered past, the noise and smoke upset them. They twitched their tails and ran!

The cows charged across the field! They broke through the fence, and crashed into the last few trucks! A coupling rod broke and half the trucks were left behind!

Edward felt the trucks jerk suddenly. But he thought they were being naughty as usual. "Those Troublesome Trucks!" he cried. "Why can't they come quietly?"

Edward had reached the next station before he realised what had happened.

News of the accident quickly reached the other engines.

"Silly Old Iron! Fancy allowing cows to break his train!" laughed Gordon. "They wouldn't dare do that to me. I'd show them!" he boasted.

Edward pretended not to mind. But Toby was cross. "Don't worry, Edward," he said. "Gordon's very mean to call you names. He doesn't know what he's talking about, cows can be very troublesome!" This made Edward feel a little better.

A few days later, Gordon rushed through Edward's station.

"Mind the cows!" he laughed, as he roared along the line. But his Driver could see something on the bridge ahead.

"Slow down, Gordon!" he said, and shut off the steam.

"Pah!" said Gordon. "It's only a cow! Shoo!" he hissed, moving slowly onto the bridge. But the cow wouldn't 'shoo'. She had lost her calf, and felt lonely.

Gordon stopped. "Be off!" he hissed. But the cow kept walking towards him and mooed even louder! Gordon was scared and backed slowly away. His Driver and Fireman tried to send the cow away. But she wouldn't move. The Guard told the Porter at the nearest station.

"That must be Bluebell," said the Porter. "Her calf is here. We'll bring it to her, now."

"Moo!" bellowed Bluebell, happily, when she saw her calf.

Gordon was very quiet on his way back to the station. He hoped no one had heard about Bluebell. But the story soon spread.

"Well, well, well!" chuckled Edward. "A big engine like you, afraid of a little cow!"

"I wasn't afraid," huffed Gordon. "I didn't want the poor thing to hurt herself by running into me."

"Yes, Gordon," said Edward, solemnly. But he knew the real reason why Gordon had stopped!

A few days later, Edward was late with the passengers for James' train. "It's Old Iron again," grumbled James. "Edward always keeps us waiting."

Thomas and Percy were annoyed. "Old Iron!" they snorted. "Why, Edward could beat you in a race any day!"

"Really!" huffed James. "I should like to see him do it."

Edward heard James as he pulled into the station, but he just smiled.

Later that week, James' Driver felt unwell. His Fireman was ringing for a relief Driver when he heard the Signalman shout.

James was puffing away without a Driver! His Fireman ran after him, but James was going too fast! The Signalman had to halt the other trains to make sure there wasn't an accident.

"Two boys were standing on James' footplate!" explained the Signalman when James' Fireman returned. "Edward is bringing the Inspector. He needs a pole, and a coil of wire rope."

James' Fireman was waiting with the pole and rope when Edward arrived. "Good man," said the Inspector. "Jump in."

"Don't worry, we'll catch him," puffed Edward.

By now, James was very frightened. He had realised that he didn't have a Driver. "I can't stop," he wailed. "Help! Help!"

"We're coming," cried Edward. And he puffed with every ounce of steam he had, until he was level with James' buffer beam.

The Inspector climbed out of Edward's cab. He had made a noose
out of the rope and tied it to the end of the pole. He was trying to
slip it over James' buffer! The engines swayed and lurched and the
Inspector nearly fell, but at last, he did it.

"Got him!" he shouted, and pulled the noose tight around
James' buffer. Then he climbed back into Edward's cab. Edward's
Driver braked gently, so he didn't snap the rope. James' Fireman
scrambled across and took control of James.

Edward and James puffed back side by side. "So 'Old Iron' caught you after all!" chuckled Edward.

"I'm sorry," whispered James. "Thank you for saving me."

When they reached the station, The Fat Controller was waiting.

"I'm proud of you, Edward," he said. "You shall go to the Works, and have your worn parts mended."

"Oh! Thank you, Sir!" said Edward, happily. "It will be lovely not to clank any more."

James' Driver soon got better and went back to work. The naughty boys had got such a shock when James started moving that they decided to wait until they were much older before trying to drive a train again.

When Edward came home, he felt like a new engine! James and all the other engines gave him a tremendous welcome. Even Gordon let out a cheer! Edward was very happy that he would never be called 'Old Iron' again!

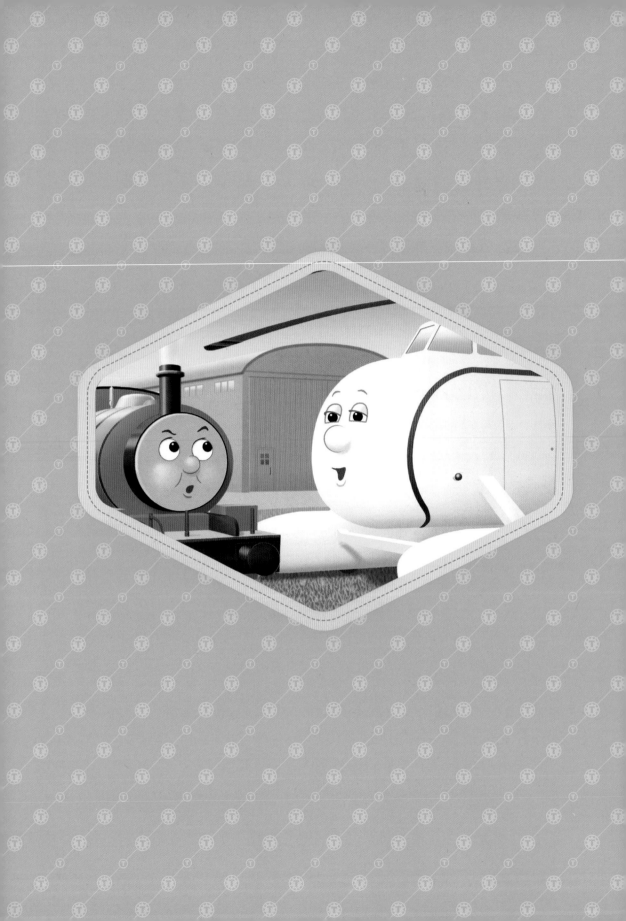

Harold and the Big Race

This is a story about Harold the Helicopter.
He thought helicopters were faster than engines
because they have propellers instead of wheels.
But then Percy challenged him to a race ...

Percy was delivering trucks of stone to the Harbour. At the Airfield nearby, there was a helicopter buzzing loudly as it waited to land.

"Loud, buzzy thing!" said Percy to his Driver. "I wish it would go and buzz somewhere else!"

The next day, Percy made a delivery to the Airfield. He stopped next to the helicopter.

"Hello," said Percy. "My name's Percy. Who are you?"

"I'm Harold," said the helicopter. "With my whirling propeller, I can fly like a bird! Don't you wish you had a propeller, too?"

"No, I like having my wheels on the rails," replied Percy, grumpily.

"You engines are much too slow," Harold continued. "With my propeller, I can go much faster than any of you!"

Percy was cross but before he could reply, Harold flew away.

Percy puffed angrily to the Quarry to pick up his next load
of trucks.

"Hello, Percy," said Toby. "You look cross. What's the matter?"

Percy told Toby what Harold had said about helicopters being
faster than engines.

"I'll show him he's wrong!" said Percy, firmly.

As Percy puffed back to the Harbour, he heard a familiar buzzing noise ahead of him.

"Look, Percy," said his Driver. "There's Harold. Let's race him! Then he'll see who's fastest!"

"Yes, we'll show him wheels are better than those funny whirling arms!" said Percy and he rushed after Harold.

Harold heard Percy speeding up behind him. He realised Percy was racing him to the Harbour.

"You'll never beat me!" he said, proudly. "I will have landed at the Airfield before you can stop at the Harbour Wharf!"

"Don't listen to him," said Percy's Driver. "We can win this!"

The race was on! Harold thought a little engine pulling heavy trucks full of stone could never beat him.

But suddenly, he saw that Percy was drawing level with him.

A few minutes later Percy's Driver shouted, "We're in the lead, Percy!"

Percy was having the time of his life, racing along faster than he had ever gone before.

"Peep! Peep! Goodbye, Harold!" he shouted as he raced ahead.

Harold looked down in surprise. He couldn't believe Percy was beating him. Harold charged after him.

Percy's Fireman was shovelling coal into the furnace as fast as he could. He wiped a cloth across his hot face.

"Phew!" he said. "This is hard work. I hope we do beat Harold!"

Then he heard the signal that warned them the Harbour Wharf was nearby.

"Nearly there!" cried Percy's Driver. "I hope we've done enough to win!"

Percy braked as he approached the Wharf. He rolled under the Main Line and halted at the buffers, puffing loudly.

"Did … we … win?" he said breathlessly.

His Fireman scrambled on to the cab roof and looked at the Airfield. "We've won!" he gasped. "Harold's still looking for a place to land!"

Percy smiled. He had shown Harold that engines are just as fast as helicopters.

Later, Harold looked embarrassed when Percy made a delivery
at the Airfield.

Percy's Driver and Fireman sang a song:

Said Harold Helicopter to our Percy, "You are much too slow!
Your Railway is out of date and not much use, you know."
But Percy with his stone trucks did the trip in record time,
And we beat Harold the Helicopter on our Old Branch Line!

Harold smiled at Percy as he flew over him. "You showed me that you can go even faster than me," he said. "I guess wheels are as good as a propeller after all!"

Percy smiled happily. What fun it had been racing against Harold. He couldn't wait to get back to the engine shed and tell the others all about it.

Annie and Clarabel, the Calmest Coaches

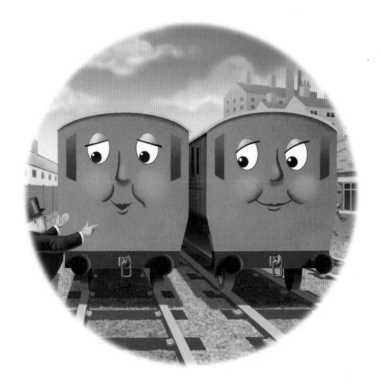

This is a story about Thomas' coaches,
Annie and Clarabel. They love running backwards
and forwards along the branch line with Thomas.
But one day, they are given a chance
to prove just how useful they can really be …

Annie and Clarabel were Thomas' coaches.

Annie could only take passengers, but Clarabel could take passengers, luggage and the Guard.

The coaches were old and in need of new paint, but Thomas loved them very much, and they loved him too.

Thomas never got cross with Annie and Clarabel, but he did get cross with other engines on the Main Line who made them late.

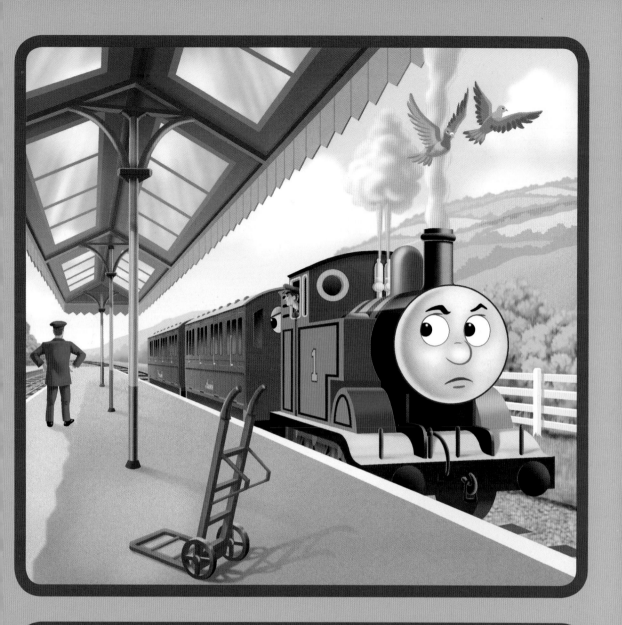

One day, Thomas, Annie and Clarabel were waiting for Henry's train to arrive. Henry was late and Thomas was getting crosser and crosser.

"How can I run my train properly if Henry is always late? He doesn't realise that The Fat Controller depends on me," he said.

"I'm sure he'll be along soon," replied Annie and Clarabel, looking around for Henry.

At last, Henry's train arrived.

Thomas was very cross with Henry. But Annie and Clarabel waited patiently as lots of passengers got out of Henry's train, and climbed into them.

Finally, the Guard blew his whistle, and Thomas started at once. But as the Guard turned to jump into Clarabel's van, he tripped over an old lady's umbrella! By the time he had picked himself up, Thomas, Annie and Clarabel were steaming out of the station!

The Guard waved his red flag to stop them, but Thomas and his Driver didn't see him. "Come along! Come along!" sang Thomas.

"I've lost my nice Guard," sobbed Clarabel.

Annie tried to tell Thomas, "We've left the Guard on the platform!"

But Thomas was too busy hurrying to listen. "Oh, come along!" he puffed impatiently. Annie and Clarabel tried to pull Thomas back, but Thomas took no notice.

Thomas didn't stop till they came to a signal.

"That silly signal! What's the matter?" Thomas asked his Driver.

"I don't know," replied the Driver. "The Guard will tell us in a minute."

They waited and waited, but the Guard didn't come.

"Peep, peep! Peep, peep! Where is the Guard?" whistled Thomas.

"We tried to tell you … we've left him behind," sobbed Annie and Clarabel.

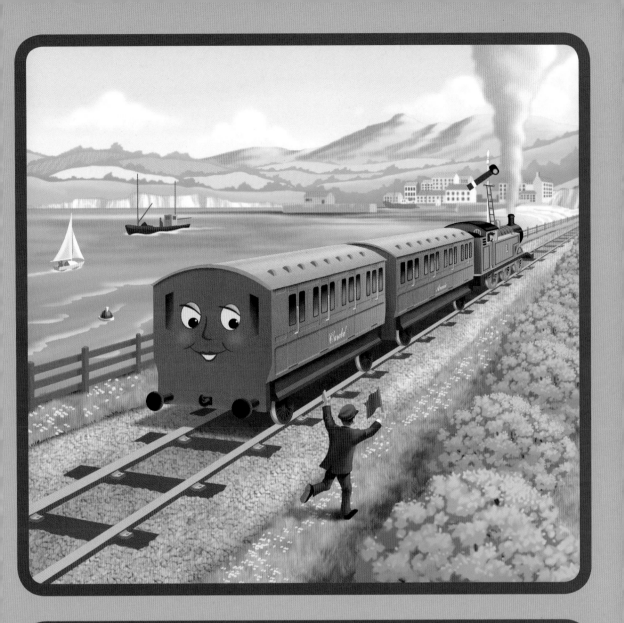

Thomas looked back along the line, and there was the Guard, running as fast as he could. Everybody cheered, especially Annie and Clarabel.

"I'm very sorry," said Thomas, when the Guard reached them.

"It wasn't your fault, Thomas. It was the old lady's umbrella," said the Guard. "The signal is down. Let's make up for lost time."

Thomas set off at once. And Annie and Clarabel sang, "As fast as you like, as fast as you like!" all the way to the end of the line.

A few days later, Thomas was ill and the Big Station couldn't make him better. He would have to go to the Works. Annie and Clarabel were sad. They would really miss Thomas.

Duck came to the station to help while Thomas was away. He was very gentle with Annie and Clarabel and they liked Duck very much.

"He is so calm with such nice manners," they told each other. "It really is a pleasure to go out with him."

They were sorry to say goodbye to Duck when Thomas came
home. But they were very pleased to have their old friend back.
They told Thomas how well Duck had managed. Thomas was a bit
jealous, but he was so pleased to be home that he soon forgot.

The Works had made Thomas feel much better, but they had left
his hand brake very stiff. This made his brakes seem as if they were
on when they weren't. Thomas' Driver and Fireman soon learnt to
be extra careful so they didn't over-run the platform.

But one day, Thomas' Fireman was ill, and a relief Fireman took
his place.

Thomas, Annie and Clarabel were waiting for Henry's train to
arrive. The Fireman fastened the coupling, but he forgot about
Thomas' hand brake. Suddenly, Thomas' wheels began to move!
Thomas, Annie and Clarabel gathered speed out of the station.

"Stop! Stop!" shrieked Annie and Clarabel, but Thomas kept
on going.

The Signalman sent a message along the line, and an Inspector prepared to stop Thomas near the Airfield. But Thomas was going much too fast for the Inspector to act.

Quickly, the Inspector climbed aboard Harold and they took off. Below, Thomas was tiring.

"I need to stop, I need to stop," he panted wearily.

Annie and Clarabel knew that they must do something to help their friend.

The coaches remembered how calm Duck was when they worked with him. They must be just as calm now. Annie and Clarabel pulled back as they went uphill and managed to slow poor Thomas down.

As they neared the next station, they saw Harold land and the Inspector run towards the platform. This time, Thomas entered the station slowly enough for the Inspector to jump into his cab, and put the hand brake on hard. Everyone breathed a sigh of relief as the train stopped.

That evening, The Fat Controller came to see Thomas, Annie and Clarabel.

He told Thomas that he would have his hand brake repaired straight away, and congratulated Annie and Clarabel for helping Thomas when he really needed them.

Annie and Clarabel were delighted, and Thomas beamed with pride. He always knew they were the best coaches on The Fat Controller's Railway!

Rheneas and the Dangerous Journey

This is the story of Rheneas, a little engine
who works high up in the mountains. Rheneas
used to moan that he never had any important
work to do, until he realised that all jobs
on the Railway are important …

One morning, Rusty stopped to talk to Rheneas, who was sitting in a siding all on his own.

"Hello, Rheneas," said Rusty. "No passengers?"

"I don't take passengers often," Rheneas said sadly. "The Fat Controller said I deserved a rest, but that was a long time ago."

Just then, Rusty's Driver came along. "Time to go and mend some tracks, Rusty," he said.

"Goodbye, Rheneas. I hope you'll cheer up soon," said Rusty.

Later that same morning, The Fat Controller came to the sheds.

"I have a very important job for you today, Rheneas," he said.

Rheneas was very surprised. "An important job!" he cried.
"Oh, thank you, Sir."

"I want you to take the children on a school trip into
the mountains," The Fat Controller explained. "I'll see you
at the Refreshment Lady's tea rooms afterwards."

"Yes, Sir," said Rheneas. But he was disappointed.

When Rheneas arrived at the station, the children and their teacher were waiting on the platform.

"A school trip into the mountains," he moaned to Rusty. "That's not an important job at all."

"Yes it is," said Rusty. "All the jobs on the Railway are important."

Rheneas didn't agree. He had seen all the sights many times before. He was worried that there was nothing exciting or important to show the children.

The Fat Controller had told Rheneas' Driver to stop at all the sights around the Island of Sodor. The first stop was the old bridge. "This bridge was built a very long time ago," his Driver announced. "It carries engines and trucks across the valley, into the mountains."

"Ooh," said the children.

But Rheneas had seen the bridge lots of times before. He didn't think it was exciting.

"Next stop is the viaduct," said the Driver.

The Driver put on the brakes and Rheneas stopped on the viaduct.

"Look at the wonderful view!" said the children together.

"You can see all over Sodor," the Driver explained.

Rheneas was still unhappy. To him, the trip didn't seem wonderful at all. "I must think of something important to show them," he puffed to himself.

Meanwhile, Rusty was busy repairing a small branch line.

The Foreman inspected the rails. He saw that the heavy rains had shifted the ground from under the tracks.

"This line must be closed until it is repaired," he said. "It is too dangerous for regular runs." He put up a sign to warn other engines not to use the line.

"Let's get to work straight away," said Rusty.

Rheneas was in a hurry as he reached the points. He had made so many stops. First, the old bridge, then the viaduct and then the lake. He was afraid he would be late for The Fat Controller.

"I'll make up time, I'll make up time," he puffed.

But the Signalmen had forgotten to switch the points. Suddenly, Rheneas found himself on the dangerous track.

"Oh, no!" cried Rheneas' Driver.

Rheneas rocketed straight past Rusty. He couldn't stop – Rheneas was out of control!

"Keep your steam up!" cried Rusty, looking worried.

"Hooray!" cheered the children, as they bumped over the tracks.

Rheneas puffed bravely up the hill. The ground was shaking beneath his wheels.

"C-courage … c-courage … c-courage," he chuffed. Then he rattled down the other side.

He was determined to deliver his passengers safely.

The children squealed in delight, as Rheneas steamed over a rickety bridge.

But their teacher was worried. She didn't like heights, and shut her eyes. Rheneas was going faster and faster along the wobbly track. His Driver gave a warning blast on the whistle. "PEEP! PEEP!"

It was the most exciting school trip the children had ever been on. "This is fun!" they cheered.

When Rheneas reached the waterfall, water splashed onto his passengers. They didn't mind at all, and laughed happily. All except the teacher.

Rheneas rocked around a tight bend and could see the station up ahead. "Not far to go ... not far to go," he chuffed.

It was such a bumpy journey that the teacher's hat flew off and blew into a field, where a goat ate it for tea!

At last, Rheneas pulled into the platform. The Fat Controller was waiting to greet him.

"That was the best school trip ever!" the children told The Fat Controller. Their teacher wasn't so sure.

"Well done, Rheneas," said The Fat Controller. "You brought your passengers back safely – that is what is important."

Rheneas beamed with pride. Now he knows that all the jobs on the Railway are important.

Rocky and
the Heavy Load

This is a story about Rocky, a new crane
who is so big that he needs an engine to pull him.
Edward and Gordon thought he was no use
– until they really needed his help …

Edward is a Really Useful Engine. He has worked on The Fat Controller's Railway for many years.

One morning, he steamed into the Docks to pick up some heavy pipes. Gordon and Thomas were already there, talking about a new crane called Rocky who had just arrived on the Island.

"He looks so strong!" Thomas puffed excitedly. "I'm sure he could lift even you up, Gordon!"

Gordon sniffed.

"That crane might be big," he said. "But he has no engine! He can't move unless one of us pulls him!"

Edward looked at the crane and saw that Gordon was right.

"Then I don't think he can be Really Useful," chuffed Edward, slowly.

"Quite right, Edward," huffed Gordon. "He will only get in the way!"

Just then, Percy arrived. He was very excited to see the
new crane!

"He will only get in the way," huffed Edward.

"New-fangled nonsense!" Gordon wheeshed. And he chuffed off.

"What's a new-funnelled nuisance, Edward?" peeped Percy.

"New-fangled nonsense, Percy!" puffed Edward, as grandly as
he could. "It's something that is new and not Really Useful."

Edward's trucks were right by the new crane.

"My name's Rocky," the crane smiled at Edward.

"I'm Edward," puffed the blue engine.

"Can I come with you?" asked Rocky. "I could help you with those heavy pipes."

"I don't need your help," sniffed Edward. "New-fangled nonsense!" And he puffed off … before the pipes had been properly tied down!

Edward was approaching a signal. He was going too fast, but he was so busy thinking about Rocky that he didn't notice.

Suddenly the signal changed to red!

Edward screeched to a stop. He jolted his trucks so much that their sides collapsed. Steel pipes toppled all over the tracks!

"Bust my buffers!" puffed Edward.

Edward looked at the heavy pipes and wondered if Rocky might help him lift them. Thomas had said the new crane was very strong.

"New-fangled nonsense!" huffed Edward.

He asked his Driver to telephone for Harvey instead. Soon the crane steamed up and started moving the pipes. But they were so heavy that he could only lift them one by one.

"This is going to take me a very long time," poor Harvey gasped.

Just then, Thomas and Emily arrived. They stopped and looked at the pipes. "We have to get through!" tooted Thomas. "Why don't you go and get Rocky?"

"No, no!" whistled Edward. "Harvey is doing a fine job. We must be patient!"

"I don't like being patient!" pouted Emily. "We have a very important job to do!"

Then they heard Gordon coming.

Gordon was rushing along very fast. He tried to stop when he saw the pipes, but it was too late. He hit them with a loud crunch, and came off the track!

It was a terrible mess. Gordon lay groaning in a pile of broken pipes.

"I can't lift Gordon!" sighed Harvey. "He's too heavy!"

"Edward!" tooted Thomas. "We need Rocky!"

Gordon looked up. "New-fangled nonsense!" he sniffed.

But Edward knew this was a disaster! Harvey couldn't possibly lift Gordon.

There was only one thing to do.

"I'll go and get Rocky!" Edward wheeshed, and raced off.

Edward steamed back to the Docks.

"Rocky, we need your help," he whistled. "It's an emergency!"

"I'm ready and waiting, Edward!" cried Rocky, happily.

So Edward buffered up to Rocky, and together they left for the junction. Everyone cheered as Edward pulled Rocky up hills and down valleys. He felt very proud to be pulling the newest arrival on Sodor.

Edward soon pulled up beside Gordon, bringing Rocky to help.

"I can fix this!" promised Rocky, smiling.

With his mighty crane arm, he lifted Gordon back onto the track.

Gordon was very surprised.

"Thank you, Rocky!" he huffed. "Good work!"

Then Rocky lifted all the pipes off the rails.

The job was done in no time!

Gordon and Edward were very impressed.

"I was silly to call you 'new-fangled nonsense'," wheeshed
Edward to Rocky. "You might be new, but you're also Really Useful.
Welcome to our Island!"

Everyone tooted and cheered for Rocky!

Jeremy and the Summer Storm

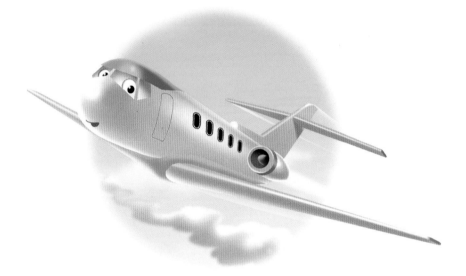

This is a story about Jeremy, a splendid jet plane,
who landed at Sodor Airport on the day
of the summer picnic. Thomas was jealous
of Jeremy until a rain storm broke out
on the Island …

Thomas the Tank Engine loves having buffers that biff and
a boiler that bubbles.

   He loves having wheels that whizz round and round and
a whistle that he can peep …

   But most of all Thomas loves working on The Fat Controller's
Railway.

It was the day of the Sodor Summer Picnic.

The Fat Controller came with news of a special job for Thomas. "You are to collect the children from the Airport, and take them to the picnic," he boomed, cheerfully.

Thomas was excited! "Yes, Sir," he whistled, and set off straight away.

The Airport was new and all the engines wanted to go there.

Thomas had just arrived, when he heard a loud noise in the sky.

"Whoosh!"

A jet plane was coming in to land!

Thomas chuffed over to the big hangar. "Hello," he peeped.
"I'm Thomas, and I'm a tank engine."

"Hello," said the plane. "I'm Jeremy and I'm a jet plane. Flying
is the most fun in the world – I can see the whole Island at once,"
he said.

Thomas thought Jeremy was being boastful. "Well, I like
travelling on tracks," he huffed.

Thomas puffed sadly away. "I never want to talk to a jet plane again!" he moaned.

He cheered up, though, when he saw the children waiting on the platform.

The Fat Controller and Lady Hatt were there, too, with a large hamper, full of delicious things to eat.

The Guard loaded the hamper into Clarabel.

Thomas set off for the picnic, but soon had to stop at a signal.

He heard Jeremy taking off. "Whoosh!"

Then Jeremy flew right over his funnel!

"It's not fair!" puffed Thomas. "Jet planes don't have to stop at signals."

At the picnic, everyone was soon having a jolly time. Everyone except Thomas.

Percy saw that he looked sad. "What's wrong, Thomas?" he asked.

"Jet planes can go wherever they like. I wish I were a jet plane," chuffed Thomas.

"But engines can pull carriages, and take children to picnics," peeped Percy. "Engines are Really Useful!" Thomas wasn't so sure.

Jeremy was jetting to the Mainland, but dark rain clouds were gathering. Jeremy had to return to the Airport.

Thomas was passing, as Jeremy came in to land. Thomas didn't want to talk to him.

"Thomas!" Jeremy called out. "A summer storm is on its way, the picnic will be ruined!"

"Cinders and ashes!" gasped Thomas. "I must tell The Fat Controller."

Thomas steamed through tunnels and whizzed round bends.
He reached the picnic just as the first drops of rain began to fall.

"Quickly!" he whooshed. "A big storm is coming. The picnic will
be washed away!"

Everyone helped pack up the picnic and boarded Annie
and Clarabel.

The children were sad that the picnic was over. Then Thomas had an idea. He steamed to the Airport, as fast as his wheels would carry him. Jeremy was inside keeping nice and dry in his big hangar.

"Please can the children have their picnic here in your hangar?" asked Thomas.

"Of course," said Jeremy. "What a splendid idea!"

Thomas was very happy.

Soon, all the children were feeling jolly again. And so was The Fat Controller.

"Well done, Thomas and Jeremy!" he boomed. "Together you have saved the picnic. You are both Really Useful!"

Jeremy was happy to have helped.

And Thomas had never felt prouder to be a tank engine.

Now, whenever Thomas sees Jeremy flying high above him in the sky, he always whistles, "peep, peep!".

And Jeremy likes nothing better than looking out for Thomas, steaming along his branch line on the Island of Sodor.

Hank and the Huffing, Puffing Engine

This is a story about Hank, a special new engine
the size of a giant! At first, the engines thought
Hank was too big for his buffers, but when Thomas
ran into trouble, they soon learned that
Hank had a big heart, too …

Hank was a brand-new engine who had just arrived on Sodor.

Hank was very special indeed. He was a very big, blue engine with bright red boiler bands.

The Fat Controller invited all the engines to welcome Hank to the Railway. When they saw how big Hank was, they gasped.

"Hank looks as strong as a giant!" peeped Percy.

"I'm sure he isn't stronger than a Sodor engine, though," Thomas puffed, proudly.

The Fat Controller had a lot of jobs for Thomas to do that day.

"First you must take new machines from the Docks to the factory," said The Fat Controller. "Then you are to pick up slate from the Quarry and deliver it to the Shunting Yard. Lastly, you must pick up an old tractor from Farmer McColl's farm and take it to the repair yard."

Hank thought Thomas must be a very important engine to have so many big jobs to do.

Hank was pleased when The Fat Controller told Thomas to show
Hank all the sights of Sodor. "You must be back by teatime for
Hank's welcome party at Tidmouth!" The Fat Controller said. "Hank
is a very special engine."

   As Thomas buffered up to the trucks that held the machines for
the factory, Hank chuffed alongside him. Hank wanted to make
friends with Thomas. "Hello there, Thomas," whistled Hank.
"You look like the finest little engine I've ever seen!"

Thomas was not very pleased to be called 'little'. "I'm a tank engine!" he huffed.

Hank saw all the heavy trucks that Thomas would be pulling. "Let me take those trucks for you!" chuffed Hank, helpfully.

"No, thank you!" peeped Thomas. "I'm strong enough to pull much heavier loads than this!" he said, and he puffed out of the Docks.

Hank hoped he hadn't hurt Thomas' feelings.

Thomas and Hank arrived at the Quarry. Hank was surprised. He was sure The Fat Controller had told Thomas to go to the factory first.

"I'm going to pick up the slate trucks," Thomas huffed.

Hank was worried. The slate trucks looked heavy, too. "Hold your huffing, Thomas!" smiled Hank. "Let big old Hank take those trucks for you." "No, thank you!" puffed Thomas, politely. "Tank engines can pull very heavy loads!"

Hank followed Thomas out of the Quarry. Thomas was heaving and huffing. Handsome Hank gleamed as he chuffed down the tracks. But poor Thomas was puffing and panting!

Hank saw children waving from the bridges. "Hello, Thomas!" they called.

"Good to see you!" Hank whooshed, happily. "My, Thomas, aren't you going to whistle 'hello'?"

But Thomas didn't have quite enough puff!

Thomas and Hank slowed at the farm, where Farmer McColl was waiting with the tractor on a flatbed trailer.

Thomas was almost out of puff. "Hello, Farmer … McColl," gasped Thomas. "This is Hank … the new engine on Sodor!"

"That's a mighty fine tractor you have!" Hank whistled, as it was coupled up to Thomas' trucks. Then he looked at Thomas. "Say, you look all puffed out! I'll take the tractor for you."

But Thomas did not want any help.

Thomas huffed and puffed but his wheels hardly turned as he tried to pull away. "Take the pressure off your pistons," Hank whistled, kindly. "Couple me up!"

But Thomas would not let Hank help him. He struggled on.

Thomas and Hank passed through a station. Some visitors waved at Thomas, but Thomas had no spare steam to whistle back!

So Hank blew a loud, long whistle for them both, which made Thomas even crosser!

Suddenly, there was trouble!

There was a FLASH and a FIZZ … a POP and a TWANG!

The loaded train was too heavy for Thomas. He had cracked a cylinder and couldn't move at all!

"Oh no!" Thomas moaned. "Now the deliveries won't be made, and you won't be back in time for your welcome party, Hank! All because I'm not a Really Useful Engine or even a very strong one!"

Hank sighed. He was sad for his new friend.

"I wanted to show you that I wasn't just a 'fine little engine'," Thomas steamed softly. "I wanted to show you how strong I am. But I need your help now, please!"

Hank was delighted to help. "You give the orders, I'll do the pushing!" he puffed. Hank coupled up to Thomas. With Hank shunting, they delivered the tractor to the repair yard together. The workmen were sorry to see that Thomas had broken down.

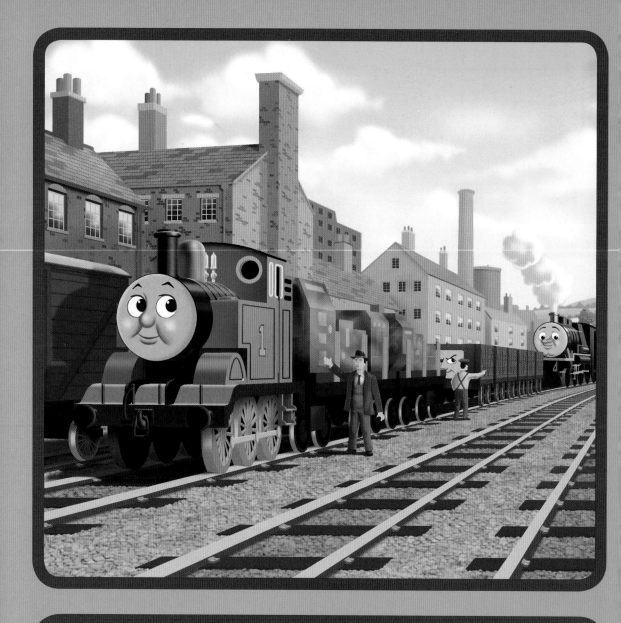

Next, Hank and Thomas chuffed into the Shunting Yard to deliver the slate trucks.

"I hope you're back on track soon, Thomas!" called the Yard Manager, as the trucks were uncoupled.

Finally, Thomas and Hank delivered the new machines to the factory. "Thank you, Thomas!" said the Factory Manager.

The engines' work was done. Hank proudly pushed Thomas all the way to Tidmouth.

WELCOME, HANK!

Thomas and Hank arrived just in time for the welcome party.

"Thank you, Hank," whistled Thomas. "Now all of Sodor knows what a strong engine you are!"

Hank smiled. "I know something, too," he said, kindly. "You're the engine everyone cheers for on Sodor. That's really something to be proud of!"

Thomas was pleased. "You *are* a special engine," he smiled to Hank, "and a very special new friend too!"